John 1-3

MATT CHANDLER

Lifeway Press®
Nashville, Tennessee

Editorial Team

Susan Hill
Writer

Jennifer Siao
Production Editor

Kyle Wiltshire
Content Editor

Jon Rodda
Art Director

Karen Daniel
Team Leader

John Paul Basham
Manager, Student Ministry Publishing

Ben Trueblood
Director, Student Ministry Publishing

Ben Mandrell
President, Lifeway Christian Resources

Published by Lifeway Press® • © 2021 The Village Church

DEWEY: 226.5

SUBHD: BIBLE. N.T. JOHN 1-3 / JESUS CHRIST / CHRISTIAN LIFE

ISBN 978-1-0877-5236-5 • Item 005834414

Unless otherwise noted, Scripture quotations are taken from the ESV® Bible (The Holy Bible, English Standard Version®), copyright © 2001 by Crossway, a publishing ministry of Good News Publishers. Used by permission.
All rights reserved.

Scripture quotations marked (MSG) are taken from THE MESSAGE. Copyright © by Eugene H. Peterson 1993, 1994, 1995, 1996, 2000, 2001, 2002. Used by permission of NavPress. All rights reserved. Represented by Tyndale House Publishers, Inc.

To order additional copies of this resource, write to Lifeway Resources Customer Service; One Lifeway Plaza; Nashville, TN 37234; fax 615-251-5933; phone toll free 800-458-2772; order online at Lifeway.com; or email orderentry@lifeway.com.

Printed in the United States of America

Student Ministry Publishing • Lifeway Resources
One Lifeway Plaza • Nashville, TN 37234

Contents

ABOUT THE AUTHOR

MATT CHANDLER serves as the lead pastor of teaching at The Village Church in the Dallas/Fort Worth metroplex. He came to The Village in December 2002 and describes his tenure as a replanting effort to change the theological and philosophical culture of the congregation.

Alongside his current role as lead pastor, Matt is involved in church-planting efforts both locally and internationally through The Village, as well as in various strategic partnerships. Prior to accepting the pastorate at The Village, Matt had a vibrant itinerant ministry for more than ten years that gave him the opportunity to speak to thousands of people in America and abroad about the glory of God and the beauty of Jesus.

Matt is the author of *Take Heart; To Live Is Christ, to Die Is Gain; Mingling of Souls; The Explicit Gospel* Bible study, *The Apostles' Creed* Bible study, and the *James* Bible study. He's also a coauthor of *Creature of the Word*.

Other than knowing Jesus, Matt's greatest joy is being married to Lauren and being the dad to their three children: Audrey, Reid, and Norah.

ABOUT THE GOSPEL OF JOHN

The Gospel of John is different from the other Gospels—Matthew, Mark, and Luke—in that more than ninety percent of its material is unique. John's Gospel does not focus on the miracles, parables, and public speaking that are so prominent in the other accounts. Instead, the Gospel of John emphasizes the identity of Jesus as the Son of God and how we, as believers, should respond to His teachings.

Of all the Gospels and any of the New Testament books, the Gospel of John most clearly teaches that Jesus is God and has always been (1:1–2, 18; 8:58; 17:5, 24; 20:28). John portrays Jesus as the eternal Word of God who became flesh to redeem people from their sins.

HOW TO USE THIS STUDY

John 1-3: The Word Became Flesh provides a guided process for individuals and small groups to walk through the Gospel of John. This Bible study book includes twelve weeks of content, each divided into two major sections: "Group Study" and "Personal Study." A leader guide is also provided to prepare those who are leading students through this journey.

GROUP STUDY

Regardless of the day of the week your group meets, each week of content begins with a group session. This group session is designed to include video teaching and group discussion.

Each group study uses the following format to facilitate simple yet meaningful interaction among students, with God's Word, and with the video teaching.

START
This section includes questions to get the conversation started, a review of the previous week's study to reinforce the content, and an introduction to the new content for the current week.

WATCH
This section includes key points from the video teaching, along with space for taking notes as students watch the video.

DISCUSS
This section includes discussion questions that guide the group to respond to the video teaching and to relevant Bible passages.

PERSONAL STUDY

Two personal studies are provided each week to take students deeper into Scripture and to supplement the content introduced in the group study. With biblical teaching and interactive questions, these sections challenge individuals to grow in their understanding of God's Word and to make practical application to their lives.

LEADER GUIDE

On pages 128-141 at the back of this book, you'll find a leader guide that will help you prepare each week. Use this guide to gain a broad understanding of the content for each week and to learn ways you can engage with students at different levels of life-changing discussion.

Under the "Start" portion of the Leader Guide, you'll find an optional ice-breaker question/activity. Feel free to use or adapt in such a way that works well for your group of students.

Through the Word

GROUP STUDY

Start
Welcome everyone to session 1.

Today we begin our study of the Gospel of John. John's Gospel differs from Matthew, Mark, and Luke (known as the Synoptic Gospels) in a variety of ways. The other three Gospels share similar language, structure, and stories. John approaches Jesus' life from a different perspective and includes accounts not found anywhere else in the New Testament. Only John's Gospel includes Jesus' "I Am" statements, the story of the Samaritan woman at the well, Jesus raising Lazarus from the dead, and Jesus' Farewell Discourse (John 14–17).

What do you hope to learn during these next 12 weeks?

John's Gospel has been described as simple enough for a child to understand and deep enough to drown an elephant. John's Gospel gives us a beautiful portrait of the person and work of Jesus Christ.

To prepare for video session 1, pray that God will help each student understand and apply this truth:

Jesus is the Christ, the Son of God, and you find life in His name.

Watch

*Use the space below to take notes while
you watch video session 1.*

Video sessions available at lifeway.com/johnbiblestudy

Discuss

*Use the following questions to guide
your discussion of the video.*

1. How does John 20:30-31 eliminate the possibility that Jesus was merely a philosopher, moral teacher, or prophet? Why is an accurate understanding of Jesus' identity crucial to our faith?

2. Jesus is the maker of all things. How does this change how you treat others?

3. John 1:1 describes Jesus as the Word. Pastor Matt taught, "The Word of God is described several times in the Old Testament as one sent forth by God to accomplish the purposes of God and then returns to God." Read Isaiah 55:11. Describe the similarities you see between this passage and how Pastor Matt described Jesus as the Word.

4. Share about a time you've been convicted, guided, comforted, or encouraged by God's Word.

THE WORD WAS GOD

If you haven't already, you soon will have to write a research paper for school. One of the keys to a good research paper is a solid thesis statement. A thesis statement declares your purpose for writing and guides the reader's expectations. Generally speaking, thesis statements usually come early in a research paper, but John revealed the purpose for his writing near the end of his Gospel.

Read John 20:30-31. Why did John write his Gospel?

John wrote his Gospel to demonstrate that Jesus is the Son of God and that by believing in Him, we may have life in His name. Understanding this thesis gives us insight as we read John's Gospel. Although his thesis comes late in the book, John addresses who Jesus is from the opening verses:

In the beginning was the Word, and the Word was with God, and the Word was God. He was in the beginning with God. All things were made through him, and without him was not any thing made that was made. In him was life, and the life was the light of men. The light shines in the darkness, and the darkness has not overcome it.
JOHN 1:1-5

Spend a few minutes reviewing the passage above. List every fact that John revealed to us about Jesus.

What stands out to you in this passage?

Matthew and Luke begin with a list of Jesus' relatives and telling the story of His birth, but John took a different approach. He began by offering proof for His thesis. In the first sentence, John revealed the main point of his book, that Jesus is the Christ, the Son of God, and that in Him is life. And this Jesus that John wrote about came to Earth, became a person just like us, and lived among us.

Spend a moment thinking about the fact that Jesus has always been, will always be, but He became a person and lived among us. Why is it significant that Jesus came to earth and lived among us?

What all did Jesus leave to come to us? Why does this matter?

God Made Visible

John was very concerned that we understand who Jesus is. The primary way we come to know God is through studying the Scriptures. When we want to know what God is like—His character, attributes, and how He responds in specific situations—we need to take a close look at how He revealed Himself in the Bible.

Read Colossians 1:15-17. How do these verses reinforce what we learned in John 1:1-5?

What does it mean for Jesus to be made in the image of the invisible God?

When we think about what God is like, often our first reaction—because of our humanity—is to believe God is disappointed, angry, frustrated, and regrets saving us. But Jesus, who is God in the flesh, shows us a very different picture. If we want to understand what God is like, we need to pay special attention to how Jesus acted in the Gospels. How did He treat sinners? The sick? The lost? What made Him angry? What made Him sad? How did outsiders respond to Him? If we want to have a thriving relationship with God, we'll have to throw out any preconceived notions about Him if they don't align with how He presented Himself in the Scriptures.

Spend a couple of minutes thinking about God. How would you describe Him? What is He like?

What do you believe God thinks about you?

What informs how you think God sees you: Your past sins or what God says about you in Scripture?

Do you have ideas about who God is that can't be confirmed by Scripture? If so, what are they?

It's hard for some of us to wrap our minds around the truth that there is a loving God who wants to have a relationship with us—despite our sinful nature and the ways we've failed Him. But Jesus is proof of that reality. Jesus is fully aware of our sins and shortcomings—it's the reason He took on flesh and came to live here on Earth—so we could be reconciled to God.

Conclude this part of this week's study by praying through the following questions.

Am I as close to Jesus as I would like to be? If not, what is holding me back?

Ask God to reveal any errors in your understanding of Him. Pray that as you explore His Word, you will learn new things about His character.

Personal Study 2
LIFE AND LIGHT

*In him was life, and the life was the light of men. The light shines
in the darkness, and the darkness has not overcome it.*
JOHN 1:4-5

A close look at John's Gospel reveals two words that appear over and over: "life" and "light." The Bible often uses the opposite of these words to describe this world's fallen nature when it speaks of "death" and "darkness." John speaks of light and life as they relate to salvation: the "light" is revelation which can lead to salvation and "life" is the spiritual life that results from salvation in Christ.

According to John, how are life and light connected to Jesus?

How does the light of Christ shine in dark places today?

Remember, John's purpose in writing was so that we might know that Jesus is the Christ, the Son of God, and that life is found in Him. Why? Because you have been made by Him and for Him. We have an invitation from Jesus to come into the life and light that He offers.

Theologian, Frederick Bruner wrote:

> We long to know who God is and what God thinks and does. In Jesus, his most personal Word, God has 'spoken' to us in the most human way possible, giving us his innermost thoughts and heart, in deeds that are as profound as his words, and the believing human race has experienced deep help ever since.[1]

Bruner wrote that "In Jesus, God has given his innermost thoughts and heart." What does Jesus' personality reveal about God?

What does Jesus' coming to Earth reveal to us about the heart of God?

Echoes of Genesis

In the first verse of John's Gospel, he declared that "In the beginning was the Word, the Word was with God, and the Word was God." These words echo all the way back to Genesis 1:

> *In the beginning, God created the heavens and the earth.*
> **GENESIS 1:1**

The life and light we read about in John have been around since before time began. Jesus is and always has been one with God. He was with God creating and sustaining the world. These passages help form our understanding of the doctrine of the Trinity—the belief that God is one in three persons.

Re-read Genesis 1:1-3 and John 1:1-5. What similarities do you see? What words and ideas appear in both places?

One of the most exciting things about the Bible is how the story unfolds over thousands of years and is conveyed through various authors. How does seeing the theme of Genesis echoed in John's Gospel help you see the big picture of Scripture more clearly?

The Light Shines On

The light shines in the darkness, and the
darkness has not overcome it.
JOHN 1:5

In the verse above the word "shines" explains that Jesus shone during His time on earth and His light continues to shine just as brightly today. At times, the darkness in today's world seems overwhelming but we can rest assured that the light of Christ has not dimmed. But if we want to live in the light of Christ, we must follow Him:

Jesus spoke to them, saying, "I am the light of the world. Whoever
follows me will not walk in darkness, but will have the light of life."
JOHN 8:12

What did Jesus promise to those who follow Him?

In what areas of your life do you need Jesus to shine light into darkness?

What is your response to Jesus' invitation to follow Him?

Close your time in prayer by asking God to shine light in areas
of darkness, confusion, and uncertainty. Give thanks to Jesus
because He continues even now shining light in dark places.

1. Frederick D. Bruner, *The Gospel of John: A Commentary* (Grand Rapids, MI: Eerdmans, 2012).

SESSION 2

God-Given Belief

GROUP STUDY

Start
Welcome everyone to session 2.

The word "believe" repeatedly appears in John's writing and is a central theme in his Gospel. What we believe is important because what we believe is foundational to who we are as human beings. We become children of God through belief. What happens when we believe? The Bible says the Spirit of God indwells us and we are transformed by His presence.

Can you recall the moment or season of life when you believed the gospel was true? What led up to it?

To prepare for video session 2, pray that God will help each student understand and apply this truth:

We become children of God by believing in Jesus' name.

Watch

*Use the space below to take notes while
you watch video session 2.*

Discuss

*Use the following questions to guide
your discussion of the video.*

1. The word "believe" appears numerous times in John's Gospel. To believe
    we have to receive the gift of belief. How is the simple act of believing a gift
    from God?

2. John 1:7 says John the Baptist came to "bear witness about the light, that
    all might believe through him." What role do we have today to bear witness
    about Jesus?

3. Pastor Matt shares how we are not born as Christians and that our par-
    ents' faith is not automatically ours. Why is it crucial for us to have a faith of
    our own?

4. Who were the people who were instrumental in telling you about Jesus?
    How did their willingness to tell you about Jesus influence you?

5. How is your life different because of your relationship with Jesus?

A MAN SENT FROM GOD

*There was a man sent from God, whose name was
John. He came as a witness, to bear witness about the
light, that all might believe through him. He was not the
light, but came to bear witness about the light.*
JOHN 1:6-8

John the Baptist is one of the most well-known people in Scripture. By any standards, his life was anything but ordinary. He was a prophet with a unique mission. His birth was miraculous; announced by an angel and born to parents well past the time when childbirth was possible (Luke 1:57-80). In his early years he lived alone in the wilderness (Luke 1:80). The focus of his ministry was, "Repent, for the kingdom of heaven is at hand" (Matt. 3:2).

Glance back at John 1:6-8. What role did John come to fill? What was the purpose of his calling?

Notice the text says, "He was not the light, but came to bear witness about the light." What does it mean to "bear witness?"

Not many of God's people were called to be prophets, but we are all called to tell others about Jesus. With that in mind, what can we learn from John the Baptist?

John the Baptist wasn't out to make a name for himself. John knew his role was to point people to Jesus. He repeatedly denied that he was the Christ and emphasized he was not the light but merely a witness to the light (1:8). John's role and our role in the kingdom are crucial. God can use any means He chooses to draw people to Himself, but He uses ordinary human beings to draw new believers to the kingdom of God.

Faith Comes From Hearing

Read Romans 10:9-17. In your own words, describe the connection between hearing the word and believing.

Glance back at verses 14-15. How should these verses impact our views on missions and telling others about Jesus?

To believe in Christ means we receive something as well. How does hearing God's Word allow us to receive and believe (v. 17)?

The gospel of Jesus Christ must be communicated for people to receive it. Certainly, God calls and equips preachers, evangelists, pastors, and teachers to communicate His Word (Eph. 4:11). But even those who aren't called to full-time vocational ministry are called to share the gospel. When we encounter Jesus and experience His presence in our lives, the most natural response is to tell others. In Scripture, the most common reaction for people who have encountered Jesus is for them to share their experience.

Read through the following passages and write down how each person responded after they encountered Jesus.

John 4:1-29. How did the woman respond in verse 29?

Mark 5:1-20. Pay special attention to verses 19-20. How did the man respond to Jesus' command in verse 19?

Acts 4:1-20. In verse 20, what did Peter and John say to the authorities?

What do these stories teach us about the value of hearing and responding to the gospel?

As believers, it's our privilege to tell other people about Jesus. We don't have to have the knowledge of our pastor or the eloquent speech of a theologian. The most effective way to communicate our faith is to share what Jesus has done for us and tell how our lives are better because He is our Lord.

Why should you consider it a privilege to tell what Jesus has done for you? What obstacles prevent you from sharing the gospel with others?

Close your time by giving thanks to God for the gift of believing. Ask Him to provide you with opportunities to share your faith. Give thanks for the people who invested in your life by sharing the gospel with you.

Personal Study 2
CHILDREN OF GOD

But to all who did receive him, who believed in his name, he gave the right to become children of God.
JOHN 1:12

Evangelism defined John the Baptist's ministry. He told people about Jesus so they would have the opportunity to believe—and in believing—God would give them the right to become children of God. All people begin in darkness, because our sins have separated us from God (Rom. 3:23). But the Bible tells us, a light has come to shine in the darkness (John 1:5). When the light of Christ shines light in the darkness—and we believe—we become children of God.

Why is it incorrect to say all people are children of God?

What's at stake for those who are not children of God?

Those who reject the light (Jesus) are not children of God. Yes, God created everyone, and therefore all human beings are made in His image (Gen. 1:27), but not everyone knows God as Father. The only path to the Father is through the Son. Jesus said, "I am the way, and the truth, and the life. No one comes to the Father except through me" (John 14:6).

You've probably heard the saying, "There are many paths to God." How does John's Gospel demonstrate this isn't true?

People who don't believe have been known to say that Jesus being the only path to God is rigid or unfair. How would you respond to that?

Son or Slave?

Jesus answered them, "Truly, truly, I say to you, everyone who practices sin is a slave to sin. The slave does not remain in the house forever; the son remains forever. So if the Son sets you free, you will be free indeed.
JOHN 8:34-36

The verses above teach that if we aren't children of God, we will be slaves to sin. Those are the only two possibilities for all of humanity. Our sin is what separates us from God, and without God's intervention, we will remain in bondage to sin. A slave has no permanent standing in God's house—only a child of God does. So, when it comes to what we believe about Jesus—what's at stake is our standing before God—and ultimately eternal life.

How should our belief in Jesus entirely define our lives?

Sin is an unpopular subject in modern-day culture. Why do you think it's difficult for some people to accept the fact that they are sinners?

How does our sin problem keep us from realizing our need for a Savior?

Fellow Heirs With Christ

*The Spirit himself bears witness with our spirit that we
are children of God, and if children, then heirs—heirs of
God and fellow heirs with Christ, provided we suffer with
him in order that we may also be glorified with him.*
ROMANS 8:16-17

**According to the verses above, what role does the Holy Spirit play in
assuring believers that they are indeed children of God?**

What does it mean to be someone's heir?

Are you confident you are a child of God? Why or why not?

If you are a child of God, you are an heir of all that God owns. Everything in this
world and in the life to come belongs to God. As a child of God, you are no longer
a slave to sin. That doesn't mean you won't struggle with sin, but it means that
God gives you the power to overcome sin, and because of Jesus' finished work
on the cross, you are forgiven of your sins.

*See what kind of love the Father has given to us, that we
should be called children of God; and so we are. The reason
why the world does not know us is that it did not know him.*
1 JOHN 3:1

*Close your time today giving thanks to God that Jesus has provided a
way to become a child of God, set free from your sins, a fellow heir with
Christ, and now you can look forward to spending eternity with Him.*

Grace Upon Grace

GROUP STUDY

Start
Welcome everyone to session 3.

During the early portion of the pandemic, there was a shortage of toilet paper all over the country. People were afraid they wouldn't have enough to last during the lockdown, so they stockpiled more than they needed. It was months before store shelves were replenished at pre-pandemic levels. This desire to hoard things that might run out or not be available comes from a scarcity mentality. Without meaning to, some of us view God with a scarcity mentality—we suspect His love and grace might run out on us or not be enough to cover our sins. So, we imagine He sits on His throne tight-fisted in a constant state of anger and disappointment in us. But by believing this, we misunderstand His character and carry a burden He doesn't want us to carry.

Do you tend to think of God as tight-fisted (angry) or open-handed (loving)? Explain.

To prepare for video session 3, pray that God will help each person understand and apply this truth:

Those who believe in the finished work of Jesus experience a well of abundant grace that never runs dry.

Watch

Use the space below to take notes
while you watch video session 3.

Video sessions available at lifeway.com/johnbiblestudy

Discuss

*Use the following questions to guide
your discussion of the video.*

1. What is the difference between a scarcity mentality and an abundance mentality?

2. How might we have a scarcity mentality with God? How does such a mentality warp our view of God and His grace?

3. How does confidence in God's grace lighten our burdens and free us from the feeling of scarcity?

4. Pastor Matt said, "What God calls us to, then, He provides for, but the primary provision God brings to us is not wealth, health, and power; it's grace." What did he mean by that statement?

5. Although the prosperity gospel isn't true, the Scriptures do teach that God is faithful to provide for our needs. Pastor Matt said, "What he calls you to, he will provide for." Have you experienced this to be true? If so, explain.

Personal Study 1
THE WORD BECAME FLESH

And the Word became flesh and dwelt among us, and we have seen his glory, glory as of the only Son from the Father, full of grace and truth.
JOHN 1:14

One of the most powerful phrases in John's Gospel is "the Word became flesh and dwelt among us" (1:14). The phrase at the end of that verse could also be translated "tabernacled among us." In the Book of Exodus, the tabernacle was the place that sat at the middle of the community where the presence and power of God dwelt among the Hebrews. From this point, they could always look up and see a pillar of clouds or fire, and they would know the presence of God was with them. Now John was saying, "The tabernacle is among us. The Word of God has put on flesh, and He is here with us."

In all other major world religions, people make attempts to get to God. In Christianity, God came to us in flesh and blood as Jesus Christ. How does this make Christianity different?

What does Jesus' coming to us teach about the heart of God?

Glance back at John 1:14 at the top of the page. What does it mean to say Jesus was "full of grace and truth"?

Why are both grace and truth necessary?

Grace and Truth

The text says Jesus is full of both grace and truth. This is excellent news for sinners. Why? Because truth without grace is cruel. On the other hand, grace without truth allows people to live in their sin and remain separated from God. But grace and truth says: "You have a sin problem that separates you from God—but by my grace I've made a way for you to be reconciled to the Father." Paul wrote,

> *For by grace you have been saved through faith. And*
> *this is not your own doing; it is the gift of God, not*
> *a result of works, so that no one may boast.*
> **EPHESIANS 2:8-9**

In a sense, the gospel is bad news before it's good news. The bad news is all people have a sin problem and have fallen short of the glory of God (Rom. 3:23). Without Jesus, there's nothing we can do to improve our standing before God. The good news is that God is full of grace, and we can be saved by grace through faith. And God's grace isn't a one-time offering—He gives grace upon grace—it includes our salvation, but it doesn't stop there (John 1:16). God's grace is an inexhaustible well that will never run dry.

Why do you think many people feel like they have to earn God's favor rather than freely accepting the grace He offers?

Do you struggle with accepting God's grace? Explain why you feel the way you do.

Why shouldn't we boast about the gift of salvation we have received through God's grace?

Born in the Likeness of Men

Have this mind among yourselves, which is yours in Christ Jesus, who, though he was in the form of God, did not count equality with God a thing to be grasped, but emptied himself, by taking the form of a servant, being born in the likeness of men. And being found in human form, he humbled himself by becoming obedient to the point of death, even death on a cross.
PHILIPPIANS 2:5-8

What stands out to you in these verses?

How do you see evidence of Jesus' grace to us in these verses?

What did it cost Jesus to be born in the likeness of men?

It was costly for Jesus to put on flesh and live among us. By taking on flesh, the all-powerful King of the universe became a man from an obscure town called Nazareth (John 1:46). Jesus came to seek and save the lost (Luke 19:10). Yet, He was despised and rejected by those He came to save. During His time on earth, He was familiar with sorrow and grief (Isa. 53:3). Ultimately, His mission led Him to a terrible death on a cross (John 19:28-30) where He died for those who had despised and rejected Him. Jesus embodied grace upon grace.

> *Close your time today in prayer by giving thanks to God that He is full of both grace and truth. Ask God to reveal if you have a scarcity mindset, and ask Him to renew your thoughts until you see that you serve a God who is full of grace.*

Personal Study 2

FROM HIS FULLNESS

For from his fullness we have all received, grace upon grace.
JOHN 1:16

You're probably familiar with the analogy that some people look at a glass of water and see it as half full, and others look at it and see it as half empty. How we mentally frame things tells us a lot about what we believe. As Christians, our goal is to align our thinking with the truths found in God's Word.

Generally speaking, do you tend to see a glass as half full or half empty? What are the pros and cons of seeing things the way you do?

According to the passage above, from Jesus' fullness we have all received grace upon grace. What do you think John meant by Jesus' fullness?

In what areas of your life are you in need of the fullness of God?

Bringing to mind and recalling various ways that God has shown His grace in our lives stirs our faith and helps us to see He will show us grace for our future needs. Jesus secured our salvation by His sacrifice on the cross. Paul wrote, "He who did not spare his own Son but gave him up for us all, how will he not also with him graciously give us all things?" (Rom. 8:32). In other words, since God has already offered us the ultimate gift in Jesus—He will continue to give us everything else we need in the future.

Do you ever worry about whether or not God will provide the grace you need? If so, what specific areas are you concerned about?

What role does prayer play in presenting your worries to God?

Think for a moment about your history with God. List a few ways He has proven Himself faithful in the past.

Grace to Help

Let us then with confidence draw near to the throne of grace, that we may receive mercy and find grace to help in time of need.
HEBREWS 4:16

According to the verse above, what do we receive when we draw near to the throne of grace? How do we access this?

Why do we tend to place limits on the amount of mercy and grace we can receive from Jesus? Why is this attitude unbiblical?

The author of the Book of Hebrews extended an astounding invitation by encouraging readers to approach the throne of grace with confidence. If you are a child of God, you don't have to come timidly to the throne. While we should certainly approach God with reverence and respect, we can simultaneously come with confidence. The Bible teaches that we can come to the throne of God and receive mercy and grace in our time of need, but we must approach the throne to ask. Prayer is a privilege that we should not neglect.

What prevents you from taking your needs to God in prayer?

After this week, do you think you have a scarcity mentality concerning God's grace? Why do you feel the way you do?

Which areas in your thought life do you need to realign with the truths found in God's Word? What passages speak to those issues?

Eugene Peterson's version of John 1:14 captures the grace and generosity of Christ:

The Word became flesh and blood, and moved into the neighborhood. We saw the glory with our own eyes, the one-of-a-kind glory, like Father, like Son, Generous inside and out, true from start to finish.
JOHN 1:14 (MSG)

Close your time in prayer giving thanks to God for the grace He has shown in your life. Ask Him to empower you to be someone who is quick to show grace to others.

The Word and the Witness

GROUP STUDY

Start
Welcome everyone to session 4.

At some point, we all wrestle with who we are as individuals. Many of us assume we find out who we are by looking within—but that's not the case. If we want to find out who we are as human beings, we have to look at ourselves in view of the God who created us.

Why do you think we learn more about ourselves as we grow in our understanding of God?

To prepare for video session 4, pray that God will help each person understand and apply this truth:

Like John the Baptist, we are able to know who we are and who we are not because we know who Jesus is.

Watch

*Use the space below to take notes
while you watch video session 4.*

Video sessions available at lifeway.com/johnbiblestudy

Discuss

*Use the following questions to guide
your discussion of the video.*

1. Pastor J. T. said, "To be an ideal witness of Christ, to learn what it looks like to grow and testify to God's work in our lives, you have to know three things: You have to know who you're not, you have to know who you are, and you can only know those two things because you know who Jesus is." Why do we have to know who Jesus is before we can make an accurate estimation of who we are?

2. In what ways was John the Baptist a good example of these qualities?

3. Why is it important to know who you aren't? How does knowing who we aren't relieve the burdens we've placed on ourselves?

4. How might culture, family members, friends, and classmates pressure us to be someone we aren't? Explain.

5. Share about a time when you realized you were trying to be someone you aren't or attempting to fill a role you couldn't fill. How did it turn out?

6. In John 1:20, John the Baptist said, "I am not the Christ." Why is it freeing to acknowledge who we are and who we aren't?

Personal Study 1
I AM NOT THE CHRIST

In session 2, we introduced John the Baptist and we'll be taking a more detailed look at John and his ministry. From John the Baptist, we can learn what it means to be a witness for Christ in a world of chaos and confusion.

Read John 1:19-28.

How would you describe John's response when the priests and Levites questioned him? (vv. 19-23)

What did John say his role was? (v. 23)

What can we learn from John the Baptist about being a witness for Christ?

People love to draw attention to themselves. We see it on TV, on social media, in school, and we undoubtedly know people who are doing everything they can to climb the social ladder. When John the Baptist began his ministry, it didn't take long before crowds were gathering to hear him preach (Matt. 3:5). Jewish authorities were curious about who he was, so they sent the priests and Levites to check him out (1:19). In spite of their scrutiny, John refused to promote himself. Instead, he denied that he was the Messiah and said his reason for coming was to point people to Jesus (1:20).

What evidence do you see in Scripture that John knew who he was but also who he wasn't?

How did John demonstrate humility?

Why is humility an essential character trait for a Christ-follower?

A Voice Crying in the Wilderness

He said, "I am the voice of one crying out in the wilderness, 'Make straight the way of the Lord,' as the prophet Isaiah said."
JOHN 1:23

John the Baptist knew who he wasn't, and he knew who he was, all because he knew who Jesus was. What does it look like for you to be a witness, to grow, and testify to God's work in your life? You have to know three things: You have to know who you're not, you have to know who you are, and you can only know those two things because you know who Jesus is.

Scripture teaches we were created by Jesus and for Jesus (John 1:3; Col. 1:16). With that in mind, why is it impossible to know who we are apart from Christ?

Name some of the outside sources we look to other than God to define who we are. Why do they lead to an inaccurate understanding of who we are and why we are here?

Growing in Knowledge of God

Author of the *Lord of the Rings* trilogy, J.R.R. Tolkien, once wrote, "So it may be said that the chief purpose of life, for any one of us, is to increase according to our capacity our knowledge of God by all the means we have, and to be moved by it to praise and thanks."[1] In other words, if you want to grow as a disciple of Jesus, and to know what it looks like to represent Him and be His disciple, you must grow in your knowledge of God.

List a couple of new things you've learned or been reminded of about God since beginning this study.

How has this growing knowledge of God provided additional insight into your own heart and character?

John the Baptist understood who Jesus was, and he knew his role was to prepare the hearts and minds of the people for His coming (John 1:23). John's knowledge about Christ motivated him to make Jesus' mission his own. One of the remarkable things about growing in our knowledge about God is the more we know about Him, the more we will love Him. As we study the Scriptures, we grow in our adoration, affection, and love of Jesus Christ, and we align our identity with His.

> *Close your time in prayer by giving thanks for the opportunity to grow in your relationship with Jesus through the study of the Scriptures. Ask God to reveal Himself to you in increasing measure.*

1 *The Letters of J.R.R. Tolkien*, Humphrey Carter, ed. (p. 400).

Personal Study 2
I AM NOT WORTHY

John answered them, "I baptize with water, but among you stands one you do not know, even he who comes after me, the strap of whose sandal I am not worthy to untie."
JOHN 1:26-27

John the Baptist is often remembered for his humility. Keep in mind, John was a normal person and therefore prone to all of the weaknesses, temptations, and failures we are capable of. When John's ministry began, and his preaching started to draw crowds, it would have been a normal human response for him to seek the spotlight for himself (Matt. 3:4-6) but nothing in the Scriptures suggests he did.

How would you describe what it looks like to be humble?

How frequently do you see humility displayed in those around you?

Name a few people you can think of who you consider to be humble. What stands out about them?

In the first-century, speculation about the coming Messiah was everywhere, so it's not surprising that the authorities questioned John about his identity (1: 19). Yet, John was quick to tell them he was not the Christ (1:20). He also denied being Elijah (1:21). John the Baptist gave us a model. In essence, John was saying: "I'm not the Christ. Don't place those expectations on me. I'm not a supernatural miracle-worker like Elijah. Don't place those expectations upon me either. I am not the Prophet. I'm simply a voice in the wilderness."

Because John knew who he was, he understood his role. When asked why he was baptizing, he said:

> *I baptize with water, but among you stands one you*
> *do not know, even he who comes after me, the strap*
> *of whose sandal I am not worthy to untie.*
> **JOHN 1:26-27**

John the Baptist was strange and misunderstood. However, he knew who Jesus was while the religious elite of his day didn't have a clue. John's knowledge of Jesus prompted him to say he was unworthy to tie His sandals (1:27). Genuine understanding of ourselves should lead us to deeper awareness of our brokenness and lead us to humility.

How does knowing Jesus help you fight the temptation to be self-absorbed and boastful?

How does a close relationship with Jesus foster humility?

Everyone has areas of weakness. What specific areas are you prone to struggle?

Life is about Jesus, not about us. John understood that Jesus was on the ultimate mission and he was called to play a supporting role. The gospel is good news, not because of who we are but because of who Jesus is. To be sure, we find our place in relationship with Him. Jesus is the focal point and everyone else plays a supporting role. What's extraordinary though, is John reflected the humility of Christ.

Christ's Example

Read Philippians 2:3-11.

According to verse 3, what motives are we to avoid when we do something for someone else?

Glance back at verses 5-7. What are some of the specific ways Jesus demonstrated humility?

How can you, like John the Baptist, model the humility of Jesus?

The whole purpose of Jesus' humility, servanthood, and sacrifice was for the glory of God. The same should be true for us. The closer we get to Jesus, the more aware we will become of how much grace we have received and how much we will continue to need. The apostle Paul asked, "What do you have that you did not receive?" (1 Cor. 4:7). If we answer that question honestly, the only appropriate response will be humility.

> *Close your time giving thanks to God for Jesus' example of humility, servanthood, and sacrifice. Ask God to reveal areas where you lack humility. Pray you will be in such close fellowship with Jesus that humility will be the result of your relationship with Him.*

SESSION 5

Behold the Lamb

GROUP STUDY

Start
Welcome everyone to session 5.

Earlier in this study, we discussed that we are created "by Jesus and for Jesus" (Col. 1:16). But the Bible teaches that because of our sinful nature, we have been separated from God. Our sin nature can be seen in our behavior, but it goes even deeper than that—sin has corrupted the nature of our hearts. God knew there was nothing we could do on our own to change ourselves so He sent His Son to save us from our sins.

Our personal sins separate us from God, but can also separate us from others. Can you think of times when this was the case?

To prepare for video session 5, pray that God will help each person understand and apply this truth:

Jesus is the Lamb of God who will defeat all sin.

Watch

Use the space below to take notes
while you watch video session 5.

Video sessions available at lifeway.com/johnbiblestudy

Discuss

*Use the following questions to guide
your discussion of the video.*

1. Read Colossians 1:21-22. In this passage, Paul says before receiving salvation in Christ, we were all "alienated and hostile in mind, doing evil deeds." Why did it take Jesus coming in the flesh to reconcile us to God?

2. Sometimes we tend to avoid the word *sin* and instead say things like "failures, short-comings, or poor choices." Why is it difficult to call sin for what it is? What do we miss by refusing to identify sin specifically?

3. At what point did you realize you had a sin problem that separated you from God? What led up to this realization?

4. What are common ways we attempt to justify our sins? Why is this foolish?

5. Last session we talked about the fact that in Christ, "we have all received, grace upon grace" (John 1:16). How is that demonstrated in Jesus' willingness to forgive past, present, and future sins?

6. Pastor Matt asked, "What stirs your affections for Jesus Christ, and what robs you of those affections?" How would you answer that question?

BEHOLD THE LAMB OF GOD

We've talked about the fact that John the Baptist was a man with characteristics that made him a powerful example of what it looks like to follow Jesus. As a prophet, his role was to prepare people's hearts and minds for Jesus' arrival. In today's session, we'll see how John responded when he saw Jesus approaching.

Read John 1:29-34.

What do you think of when you hear the term Lamb of God?

Why is it noteworthy that John the Baptist called Jesus "the Lamb" instead of "a lamb"?

John said Jesus' reason for coming was to "take away the sins of the world." With this in mind, why is it foolish to attempt to minimize or hide our sins from Jesus?

In our current place in history, the phrase, "Lamb of God" doesn't resonate in the same way it did when John the Baptist first spoke those words. To the Jews who heard those words, "the lamb" meant everything. The title "Lamb of God" derives from the theme of Passover (Ex. 12; 29) and the Suffering Servant passages in the Book of Isaiah:

He was oppressed, and he was afflicted,
yet he opened not his mouth;
like a lamb that is led to the slaughter,
and like a sheep that before its shearers is silent,
so he opened not his mouth.
ISAIAH 53:7

How did this prophecy of Christ written by the prophet Isaiah become reality in Jesus' life and ministry? Give specific examples.

In the Old Testament, there had to be a shedding of blood for the covering of sins, which was done through sacrificing animals. How does this connect to what Jesus did for us on the cross?

The Iniquity of Us All

In the Old Testament, animal sacrifices had to be offered over and over again. Jesus came to deal with sin once and for all. It's significant that John the Baptist didn't refer to Jesus as "a lamb of God" but "the Lamb of God." Jesus was the one who God appointed to be the final sacrifice for sin. Although we were the guilty party, God sent Jesus to die in our place. The prophet Isaiah said,

All we like sheep have gone astray; we have turned—every one—to
his own way; and the LORD has laid on him the iniquity of us all.
ISAIAH 53:6

Understanding now what the Lamb of God means, how do these passages from Isaiah help you understand Jesus?

Think about the fact that Jesus willingly took on the sins of humanity— including yours. What emotions does that provoke in you?

The author of the Book of Hebrews wrote, "For it is impossible for the blood of bulls and goats to take away sins" (Heb. 10:4). There's an old saying, "God helps those who help themselves." However, nothing could be further from the truth. Jesus came to do what we could not do for ourselves. We could not eliminate our sin problem, and the animal sacrifices of the Old Testament didn't have the power to save people from their sins. Only Jesus can save, and He did. Hebrews says:

> But when Christ had offered for all time a single sacrifice for
> sins, he sat down at the right hand of God, waiting from that
> time until his enemies should be made a footstool for his feet.
> **HEBREWS 10:12-13**

Jesus made a once and for all sacrifice for our sins—but it was costly. How does considering the great cost of His sacrifice help you better appreciate the grace you have received?

*Close your time in prayer by confessing your sins to God
and asking for forgiveness. Give thanks that because
of Jesus' sacrifice you can be reconciled to God.*

Personal Study 2
REMAIN AND ABIDE

And John bore witness: "I saw the Spirit descend from
heaven like a dove, and it remained on him.
JOHN 1:32

Jesus came not only to take away the sins of the world (past tense), but to continue to take away our sins. John the Baptist could've said, "Behold, the Lamb of God who's *continuing* to take away the sins of the world." Not only is this a present and ongoing action, but so is the abiding power of the Holy Spirit. The verse above says the Spirit remained on Jesus. Likewise, if we are children of God, the Holy Spirit remains with us (Rom. 8:9). In this way, we begin to get a sense of what the Christian life is. Receiving eternal life and the forgiveness of our sins is only the starting point of our life with Jesus.

Do you know anyone who became a Christian and nothing really changed about them? Why is this an inaccurate picture of what it means to follow Christ?

What changes about our lives when we continue to remain in Jesus?

Jesus came to take away the sins of the world but seeking His forgiveness for our sins is the starting point and not the final destination. God intends for His people to abide in Jesus, and learn what it means to experience life at it's finest. Jesus said, "The thief comes only to steal and kill and destroy. I came that they may have life and have it abundantly" (John 10:10). Abiding in Jesus doesn't mean we don't have problems—Jesus said that we should expect them (John 16:33). But if we abide in Christ, we can anticipate His peace, help, and joy regardless of the circumstances we are going through.

What Does it Mean to Abide?

Read John 15:4-11.

Glance back at verse 4. What metaphor does Jesus use? What does this teach us about life with Christ?

What does it look like to abide in Jesus on a daily basis?

What are some of the common obstacles you face that prevent you from abiding in Christ?

Jesus was a master teacher and He often communicated by using analogies that were well-known to His audience. In the society familiar with farming that Jesus lived in, it's not surprising that He spoke about plants and used the example of a vine and branch. Jesus' teaching style often included using familiar examples to teach unfamiliar spiritual truths. On it's own, a branch doesn't possess what it needs to survive—it relies on the vine to supply the resources it needs to grow and flourish. In the same way, apart from Christ, God's people don't have what it takes to live the Christian life—we must remain closely connected to Jesus—relying on Him to bear fruit.

Have you experienced a time of abiding in Christ and then got sidetracked? What differences do you notice between times of abiding compared to when you're not?

Glance back at verse 5. According to Jesus, when it comes to our spiritual life, how much can we accomplish without Him? Is this hard for you to accept? Why or why not?

Christ promises that those who abide in Him will bear fruit. What does it look like for you to bear fruit?

The apostle Paul described the fruit of the Spirit this way:

> *But the fruit of the Spirit is love, joy, peace, patience, kindness, goodness, faithfulness, gentleness, self-control; against such things there is no law.*
> **GALATIANS 5:22-23**

How would your life be different if you prioritized abiding in Jesus above everything else?

What steps can you take to make abiding in Jesus a priority in your daily life?

Close your time today asking Jesus to help you abide in Him. Give thanks to God that because of His grace He's given you the opportunity to know and fellowship with Him.

Called to Follow

GROUP STUDY

Start
Welcome everyone to session 6.

Being invited to do something is fun. Things we might be invited to include birthday parties, weddings, family reunions, the prom, graduations, or any manner of social gatherings. Invitations to things vary, but the common characteristics that come with invitations are who, what, when, where, and why. In this session, we'll see that Jesus issues an invitation for us to follow Him, and He invites us to "Come and see" (John 1:39).

If you were speaking to someone unfamiliar with Jesus, what would you tell them about following Him?

To prepare for video session 6, pray that God will help each person understand and apply this truth:

Jesus continues to draw followers to Himself in the same ways He drew His first disciples.

Watch

Use the space below to take notes
while you watch video session 6.

Discuss

*Use the following questions to guide
your discussion of the video.*

1. How would you describe the difference between believing Jesus exists and following Him as Lord? How do people get the two confused?

2. Jesus asked two disciples of John the Baptist, "What are you seeking?" (John 1:38). Why is this an important question for all of us to answer?

3. Name a few of the ways your life is different because you follow Jesus.

4. What role have fellow believers played as you have followed Jesus? How would things be different without them?

5. Who might you invite to come and follow Jesus alongside you? Set aside some time this week to pray for these individuals.

Personal Study 1
WHAT ARE YOU SEEKING?

Since the beginning of Jesus' ministry people have been confused and conflicted about His identity. In the first-century, people wondered if He was the Messiah. Numerous theories about His identity circulated widely. When John the Baptist came face-to-face with Jesus he was quick to proclaim who Jesus was saying, "Behold, the Lamb of God!" (John 1:36). In this biblical account two of John's disciples started following Jesus:

> *The two disciples heard him say this, and they followed Jesus. Jesus turned and saw them following and said to them, "What are you seeking?" And they said to him, "Rabbi" (which means Teacher), "where are you staying?" He said to them, "Come and you will see." So they came and saw where he was staying, and they stayed with him that day, for it was about the tenth hour.*
> **JOHN 1:37-39**

What did Jesus ask them? Why is this a question we all have to answer?

These two asked Jesus where He was staying. How did Jesus respond? What does Jesus' response tell us about His nature?

Notice, Jesus asked them, "What are you seeking?" People come to Jesus for a variety of reasons, but those who want to be His followers need to count the cost of discipleship. Jesus never sugarcoated what it might cost to follow Him. In Luke's Gospel, a potential Christ-follower said he'd follow Jesus and Jesus warned that if he did so he might wind up homeless: "And Jesus said to him, 'Foxes have holes, and birds of the air have nests, but the Son of Man has nowhere to lay his head'" (Luke 9:58). Jesus never promised that following Him would be easy. On the contrary, He told His followers to expect opposition (John 15:18-25).

Think for a moment about your relationship with Jesus. What are you seeking? Describe the kind of relationship you want with Him.

Are you willing to follow Jesus on His terms? Why or why not?

What evidence have you seen that following Jesus is worth the cost?

Come and You Will See

When these two asked Jesus where He was staying He said, "Come and you will see" (John 1:39). They took Jesus up on His invitation and spent the day with Him. During the time of Jesus' earthly ministry, teaching included learning from a rabbi's spoken words but it wasn't limited to verbal teaching. Disciples followed a rabbi or teacher and learned from his daily habits and lifestyle. Jesus' intention is never for His followers to merely know about Him—He invites us into a lifestyle of knowing Him personally.

What is the difference between knowing about someone and personally knowing them?

Think about the people you know the best. How did you get to know them well?

What are the main things that prevent you from growing in your relationship with Jesus?

Why do we sometimes confuse knowing about Jesus for actually knowing Jesus?

How is it possible for modern-day believers to know Jesus well?

Jesus' invitation to follow Him isn't a lifetime offer of dead religion. Jesus invites us into a living and thriving relationship. Since this is possible, we shouldn't settle for anything less. As believers today, we follow Christ by studying and obeying the Scriptures, cultivating a lifestyle of devoted prayer, and being active members of a biblical community in a local church. There's a massive difference between believing Jesus exists and following Him as Lord. And there's a difference between knowing about Jesus and following Him so closely we recognize His voice. Jesus said, "My sheep hear my voice, and I know them, and they follow me. I give them eternal life, and they will never perish, and no one will snatch them out of my hand" (John 10:27-28).

> *Close your time today by telling Jesus what you are seeking from Him. Tell Him the kind of relationship you want to have. Ask Him to teach you to follow so closely that you easily recognize His voice.*

Personal Study 2
FOLLOW ME

*The next day Jesus decided to go to Galilee. He
found Philip and said to him, "Follow me."*
JOHN 1:43

In the first century, it was customary for a disciple to take interest in a rabbi and choose to follow him. The relationship depended on the disciple's motivation to attach himself to a rabbi's ministry. Jesus differed in His approach by taking the initiative and extending an invitation. He said to Philip, "Follow me" (1:43). This approach reflected the goal of Jesus' mission. Luke said, "For the Son of Man came to seek and to save the lost" (Luke 19:10).

Why is it significant that Jesus initiates relationships with His disciples?

If Jesus initiates the relationship, what responsibility do we have to take? Explain.

The Bible makes it clear that Jesus initiates relationships and issues an invitation for people to follow Him. But a response is required on our part. To ignore Jesus' invitation is the equivalent of refusing Him. In Luke's Gospel, Jesus revealed what it looks like to follow Him:

*And he said to all, "If anyone would come after me, let him
deny himself and take up his cross daily and follow me. For
whoever would save his life will lose it, but whoever loses
his life for my sake will save it. For what does it profit a man
if he gains the whole world and loses or forfeits himself?*
LUKE 9:23-25

What do you think Jesus meant when He said His followers are to "deny themselves?" How does this message differ from what we routinely hear in our culture?

For the first disciples, there was a significant risk in following Jesus. What are the risks today of following Him?

How do the risks in America differ from what Christians experience in other parts of the world?

Following Jesus requires self-denial because we are no longer living for ourselves and our agenda. Christ-followers are focused on Jesus and an agenda that serves the kingdom of God. Jesus said a Christ-follower is to "take up his cross daily and follow me" (v. 23). In Roman culture, the cross was the most excruciating form of execution. So, by saying that we are to "take up our cross," Jesus was saying we must be willing to be subjected to painful circumstances because of our allegiance to Him.

What did Jesus mean when He said, "For whoever would save his life will lose it, but whoever loses his life for my sake will save it" (v. 24)?

How is it possible to gain the whole world and lose yourself? (v. 25).

In all four Gospels, there's a common theme that communicates a Christ-follower must lose his life to save it (John 12:25; Luke 14:26-27, 17:33; Matt. 10:38-39, 16:24-25; Mark 8:34-35). The point is, Christians must abandon their devotion to this broken world and go all in for Christ and His mission. No matter how much wealth, privilege, or success someone gains in this lifetime; a person will find himself eternally penniless if he dies apart from Christ.

Notice that Jesus said we are to take up our cross "daily." How do you practice this in your daily life?

Dying to self isn't something we can do in our own power. How do you rely on Jesus to live out this teaching?

What are common reasons people might hold out from going "all in" following Jesus?

Close your time today by asking God to empower you to live the kind of life that John's Gospel describes. Tell Him your fears and reservations. Ask Him for the type of relationship with Jesus that makes the costs more than worth it.

SESSION 7

New Wine

GROUP STUDY

Start
Welcome everyone to session 7.

In this session, we'll explore Jesus' first miracle at a wedding in a town called Cana. This first miracle—which John refers to as a "sign"—represents the reality that the old way had passed and a new way had come (John 2:11). New beginnings are exciting, but for many of us, our temptation is to fall back into familiar patterns and old habits.

Have you ever asked why something was done a certain way and heard the response, "Because that's how we've always done it." Why is this a poor reason?

To prepare for video session 7, pray that God will help each person understand and apply this truth:

The first sign of Jesus' ministry reminds us that the old has passed away and the new has come.

Watch

*Use the space below to take notes
while you watch video session 7.*

Video sessions available at lifeway.com/johnbiblestudy

Discuss

*Use the following questions to guide
your discussion of the video.*

1. How does our relationship with Christ (vertical relationship) influence our relationships with others (horizontal relationships)?

2. Pastor Matt said, "If you pay attention to your frustrations and agitations, they are almost always tied to thinking life is about you." Do you find this to be true? How have you experienced it to be true?

3. What does having a servant's heart look like? How does this mentality differ from what our culture teaches?

4. Jesus' first miracle conveyed the reality that the old had passed away, and a new way had come. What are some "old ways" you might still be holding onto despite having a new life in Christ?

Personal Study 1

THE WEDDING AT CANA

Read John 2:1-12.

Throughout the Gospel of John, the author refers to Jesus' miracles as "signs." John wanted to communicate that Jesus didn't perform miracles just because He was able. Rather, Jesus was pointing people to something greater. Jesus' miracles demonstrated He had been sent by the Father. His signs authenticated His identity as the Messiah they'd been anticipating (Luke 7:22).

In these verses, we find Jesus at a wedding. What does it tell us about Jesus that He was invited to and attended social gatherings?

How would you describe Jesus' response when Mary told Him the wine had run out?

Why would Jesus resist Mary? What did Jesus mean when He said His hour had not yet come?

In the Middle East, hospitality was, and still is, taken seriously. Running out of drinks would've been an embarrassing situation. Mary went to Jesus to solve the problem and spare the wedding party from public embarrassment. Jesus' response to Mary may seem out of character, but it signaled a turning point. This was Jesus' first miracle. He was revealing Himself in a public way, doing what the Father would have Him do. Mary, and everyone else's requests were less important than the Father's plan. "My hour" refers to the hour of Jesus' glorification where His identity would be fully revealed. The fact that Jesus ultimately did what Mary asked, shows His initial response was a statement of His priorities rather than a rejection of Mary's request.

Why should we seek to prioritize our obedience to the Father over the wishes of others?

Have you ever obeyed God and disappointed a family member or friend because of your obedience? If so, what did you learn?

Glance back at verse 5. How did Mary respond to Jesus? What can we learn from her?

A New Way

For the Jews of this day, any moral or physical blemish made one unclean and unfit to be in the presence of God until there was a rite or ritual of ceremonial cleaning that restored fellowship with God. Jesus, in this act of transforming water in purification jars into wine, was replacing that old model with something new. Jesus began His ministry with a sign that displayed His glory and drew onlookers to see that Jesus and the new kingdom had arrived.

How did the disciples respond to Jesus' signs (v. 11)? How should we respond to Jesus' work in our own lives?

John made it clear that Jesus' disciples saw His miracle and came to faith in Him (2:11). For a modern audience, it's important to realize that all of Jesus' "signs" were designed to point to His power and affirm He is God.

Why do new ways of doing things tend to throw us off balance?

How might we embrace the new work Jesus is trying to do in and through us?

Seeing the new work of Jesus should always result in belief and new life. Jesus' ministry, and this miracle specifically, had brought a new era of redemptive history where what was coming would be much better than what came before. The old had passed and the new had come. Jesus announced a new way founded in His redemptive work (John 14:6).

> *Close your time giving thanks to God that the old has passed and the new has come.*

Personal Study 2
A NEW CREATION

Read 2 Corinthians 5:17-21.

Jesus didn't just come to change the sacrificial system and purification rites of the Old Testament—Jesus came to change the hearts and minds of people and to give us a new nature. Our relationship with Jesus changes us and makes us a new creation. As we are changed by Jesus, our relationship with Him changes our relationship with other people.

Glance back at verse 17. What is true of everyone who is "in Christ?"

How has God reconciled us to Himself through Christ?

In this passage, Paul referred to God's people as "ambassadors for Christ." What does it mean to be an ambassador for Christ?

A New Role

An ambassador is a diplomat who represents and advocates for the interest of a nation or an organization. An ambassador for Christ is a citizen of the kingdom of heaven who uses their Spirit-given abilities to advocate for Jesus. At first glace, this role may seem intimidating. But before we get stressed, we have to remember that a Christian lives out of the overflow of abiding in Jesus. We aren't called to be superhuman—we are called to abide in Jesus and trust Him to equip us to do what we can't accomplish in our own strength. Success in our role is dependent on Jesus, not on our skills or abilities.

List a few ways you can be an "ambassador for Christ" with your friends and family.

How does your relationship with Jesus influence your relationships with your parents or guardian? Your friends? Your teachers?

Being an ambassador for Jesus is not a call to be unnaturally religious. God's Word reveals to us that we cannot work our way to a right relationship with Him, but that we must come to Him in faith and abide in Him. Genuinely abiding in Jesus, knowing Jesus, loving Jesus, and growing in relationship with Jesus transforms us in such a way that there is a kindness, life, and joy in us that other people are naturally drawn to and want to be around.

How would you describe the difference between being "unnaturally religious" and a person who abides in Jesus?

Paul said, "we are ministers of reconciliation" (2 Cor. 5:18). Even as a teenager, how can you be a minister of reconciliation?

A New Motive

Obedience to God and service to others are two markers of someone who has been reconciled to God and taken on the role of an ambassador for Christ. Prior to becoming Christ-followers, we prioritized self-interest above everything else. But as people who have been reconciled to God we no longer look to our own self-interest, but rather, God's glory is the driving motivation behind everything. Paul wrote:

> *I have been crucified with Christ. It is no longer I who live, but Christ who lives in me. And the life I now live in the flesh I live by faith in the Son of God, who loved me and gave himself for me.*
> **GALATIANS 2:20**

How does believing the gospel help us overcome our natural inclination toward self-interest?

What desires or motivations has Christ helped you crucify?

The miracle at the wedding in Cana revealed change had arrived. The change continues as God transforms people through the gospel of Jesus Christ. We are a new creation with a new motivation driven by the work of Christ in our lives.

> *Close your time today asking God to help you be an effective ambassador for Christ.*

The Temple, Spiritual Consumerism, and Jesus

GROUP STUDY

Start
Welcome everyone to session 8.

The last several sessions have taken a close look at John's Gospel and examined passages that reveal insights about Jesus' identity. In this session, continue to take a closer look at who Jesus is and what He does.

How would you describe the difference between what someone does and who they are?

To prepare for video session 8, pray that God will help each person understand and apply this truth:

John reveals what Jesus does in order to show us who Jesus is: a prophet who confronts us, a priest who cleanses us, and a king who constructs the temple of true worship.

Watch

*Use the space below to take notes
while you watch video session 8.*

Video sessions available at lifeway.com/johnbiblestudy

Discuss

*Use the following questions to guide
your discussion of the video.*

1. Spiritual consumers put themselves at the center of worship, not God. What does this look like today? How can we avoid being spiritual consumers?

2. How would you describe the holiness of God to a non-believer or someone who is a new Christian?

3. Why should God's holiness call us to worship with reverence and awe?

4. Pastor J. T. said, "Consumer Christianity will tell you Jesus is merciful, but it won't tell you He's holy." Why must we be mindful that Jesus is both merciful and holy?

Personal Study 1

CLEANSING THE TEMPLE

Read John 2:13-22.

What did Jesus witness in the temple?

Are you comfortable with Jesus' response to what He saw in the temple? Why or why not?

Why did this particular kind of commerce make Jesus so angry?

To celebrate Passover, Jews from surrounding areas traveled to Jerusalem. While there, every participant was required to sacrifice an animal. For those who had traveled a long distance, it was difficult to bring their livestock with them. It was much more convenient to purchase their animal to sacrifice once they arrived in Jerusalem. Early on, the commerce booths were set up outside a good distance from the temple. But by Jesus' time, the outer court, which was supposed to be a place of prayer and worship for all people, had been converted into a place for buying and selling. The people who had come to worship disrespected God for the sake of convenience.

Where do you think they went wrong in their pursuit of convenience?

A Prophet Who Confronts

Jesus wasn't angry because they we offering a sacrifice or purchasing it once they arrived in Jerusalem. Jesus was angry because they were buying and selling in the temple. He's not challenging the commerce of the day or forbidding convenience. He was challenging the fact that the commerce was happening in the temple. People had traveled all that way to worship and they missed the point because they were putting their convenience at the center of the experience and disrespecting the house of God. The lack of reverence Jesus saw made Him so angry that He made a whip of cords, turned over tables, and He drove them out of the temple.

What are some ways we subtly or directly choose convenience over authentic worship of God?

Is it possible for something to begin as well-intentioned but turn into something offensive to God? Can you think of any examples?

What does this passage reveal about how we should worship God?

What responsibility should we take to examine our own practices and determine if they might unintentionally be dishonoring to God?

Challenging the Status-Quo

*His disciples remembered that it was written, "Zeal
for your house will consume me."*
JOHN 2:17

Jesus' disciples watched what was taking place and remembered the words
David had written centuries before: "For zeal for your house has consumed me,
and the reproaches of those who reproach you have fallen on me" (Ps. 69:9). As
the disciples watched Jesus clear the temple, they connected His zeal to the
zeal David had expressed. The sacred space that had been set apart for worship
had become chaotic for the sake of convenience—and Jesus wasn't having it—
because it had negatively influenced the people's ability to worship.

What does this account reveal to us about prioritizing worship?

**How would you describe your quality of worship at this stage in life?
What adjustments might you need to make?**

Worship is a crucial aspect in the life of a Christian. To understand who Jesus is,
we must recognize that He prioritized worship and had a deep passion for the
house of God. Worship isn't something we should ignore or approach casually.
God's people are called to worship with reverence and intentionality. Like the
worshipers at the temple, we should welcome Jesus' challenge to the status quo
so that we are worshiping God whole-heartedly.

> *Close your time by asking God to help you worship
> with reverence and awe. Spend time praising Him
> for who He is and the goodness of His nature.*

Personal Study 2
A PRIEST WHO CLEANSES

For we do not have a high priest who is unable to sympathize with our weaknesses, but one who in every respect has been tempted as we are, yet without sin.
HEBREWS 4:15

Read the above passage slowly. List every detail it reveals about Jesus.

How does understanding that Jesus sympathizes with our weaknesses help us have a close relationship with Him?

Jesus is a prophet who confronts sin, but He's also a priest who cleanses us from sin. The Bible refers to Jesus as our "high priest" (Heb. 4:15). In the Old Testament, one of the primary responsibilities of the priest was to cleanse the temple and make sure it was prepared to receive people for worship. But in John 2:13-25, we see the priests had failed to do their job by allowing the temple to become a place of commerce. So, Jesus, the true Priest, came in and cleaned up the temple, ridding it of filth and ungodliness.

Why was it loving of Jesus to drive the money-changers out of the temple? What was He trying to teach them?

Can you recall a time when Jesus brought to your attention a sin you didn't realize you were committing? If so, what happened?

Jesus wants to cleanse us from all sin—the ones we are aware of and the ones we don't even know about. The text says "he drove them all out" (2:15). That might sound harsh, but in reality Jesus was demonstrating mercy rather than judgment. It would be judgment if the text said, "He left them there in their sin." Jesus was showing mercy by calling attention to their sins and giving them the opportunity to repent and reprioritize worship above everything else.

A King Who Constructs a Temple of Worship

So the Jews said to him, "What sign do you show us for doing these things?" Jesus answered them, "Destroy this temple, and in three days I will raise it up."
JOHN 2:18-19

Why did the Jews question Jesus about what He did in the temple?

What was Jesus referring to when He said, "Destroy this temple and in three days I will raise it up"? How was this later fulfilled?

The Jews were offended by Jesus' actions in the temple because He was exerting authority they wanted to keep for themselves. They asked Jesus for a sign to prove His authority and Jesus refused to give them one (v. 18). Jesus didn't perform miracles on demand for anyone. Instead, He once again referred to His death, burial, and resurrection. The Jews were attempting to control Jesus, which is impossible. Spiritual consumers want a sign from Jesus; disciples just want Jesus. The Jews demanded an immediate sign, but He delayed until the resurrection, because God does not operate on our timetable.

What is the difference between wanting something from Jesus and wanting Jesus?

We often think we want a god we can control but why would a god who we could control not be God at all?

List ways Jesus offers something better than spiritual consumerism.

What we've seen unfold in the temple is a conflict between spiritual consumerism and true worship, and the only answer to spiritual consumerism is a better view of Jesus. Jesus reveals Himself as a prophet, a priest, and a king. As true worshipers of God, we will be more enthralled with who Jesus is than what He does. As Christians, we have the privilege of knowing Jesus—not just what He does for us—but who He is. There is no higher honor.

> *Close your time today by thanking God that Jesus reveals Himself as a prophet, priest, and king. Tell Him you want to worship Him for who He is and savor His lordship.*

An Inadequate Faith

GROUP STUDY

Start
Welcome everyone to session 9.

With so much media and technology at our fingertips, we can learn more about people than ever. If you're a fan of a specific artist or celebrity, there's a good chance you know about their work, what they are working on next, and even details about their personal life. But knowing factual information about someone is very different than having a relationship.

Who are the people who know you the best? How did you get to know them so well?

Knowing facts about someone and knowing them personally are two totally different things. We may feel like we know our favorite actors, singers, or athletes, but all we really know is things about them. Tragically, this is the type of relationship many have with Jesus. They know things about Him, but they don't really know Him.

To prepare for video session 9, pray that God will help each person understand and apply this truth:

The Gospel of John encourages us to examine our relationship with Jesus and ensure that we know Him personally rather than simply knowing information about Him.

Watch

*Use the space below to take notes
while you watch video session 9.*

Video sessions available at lifeway.com/johnbiblestudy

Discuss

*Use the following questions to guide
your discussion of the video.*

1. What is the difference between loving God and attempting to use Him to get what you want?

2. In this week's Scripture passage, the people loved the signs (miracles) Jesus was doing, but they didn't love Jesus. What are some examples of how people do this today? Why is this approach dangerous to you and a threat to the church?

3. We all want to be blessed by God. How can you tell if you truly love Jesus apart from His blessings?

4. Pastor Matt said, "The good news of the gospel of Jesus Christ is not that if you give your life to Jesus everything goes the way you want it. It's that regardless of what comes, Jesus will be there and you will find Him to be enough." How have you found this to be true in your own life?

Personal Study 1
TRUE FAITH

Now when he was in Jerusalem at the Passover Feast, many believed in his name when they saw the signs that he was doing. But Jesus on his part did not entrust himself to them, because he knew all people and needed no one to bear witness about man, for he himself knew what was in man.
JOHN 2:23-25

What led the crowds to "believe" in Jesus? How would you describe their faith?

What does Jesus' response to their "belief" reveal to us about who He really is?

Unlike the rest of us, Jesus cannot be tricked by flattery or lured by praise. He knows what's in people's hearts and He understood that the people referred to in the above passage were enthralled with what He was doing rather than His identity as the Son of God. They weren't interested in who He was but what He could do for them. As a result, Jesus didn't "entrust Himself" to them (v. 24) meaning Jesus withheld revealing His true identity to them because of their inauthentic faith.

What is the difference between simply believing in God and believing that Jesus is Lord?

How do we confuse the two?

Many people know facts about Jesus without having a relationship with Him. These people have no intention of ever following Him. They just know some things about Him. True believers love and trust Jesus in every area of their lives. True belief produces fruit.

What kind of characteristics accompany someone who loves and trusts Jesus?

When did your own faith change from knowing about Jesus to truly following Jesus?

Evidence of Saving Faith

Many claim the Christian faith but far fewer live as authentic followers of Jesus. To be sure, we all sin and fall short of the glory of God even after we become believers (Rom. 3:23). Even people who love Jesus above all things have days (or weeks) when they completely miss the mark. But the Bible teaches that people who love and trust Jesus live in a way that makes them distinct. Jesus said:

"If you love me, you will keep my commandments."
JOHN 14:15

How does obedience to Jesus make a Christian distinct from the world around them?

What might it mean if someone claims to love Jesus, but constantly lives a lifestyle that is contrary to His Word?

What new insight do these verses give to change the way you think about obedience?

Jesus made it clear: If we love Him, we will obey Him—not because we are forced to—but because we want to. When we truly love God, our desires start to align with His will for our lives. We begin to want the same things He wants and have a desire to live a life that brings Him glory. It doesn't mean we will be perfect—far from it. Jesus is the only One who is without sin. But if we love Jesus, we will experience a desire to obey His Word and will feel conviction when we disobey Him. The author of Psalm 119 wrote:

> *Teach me, O LORD, the way of your statutes;*
> *and I will keep it to the end.*
> *Give me understanding, that I may keep your law*
> *and observe it with my whole heart.*
> *Lead me in the path of your commandments,*
> *for I delight in it.*
> **PSALM 119:33-35**

These words by the psalmist were not written by a man who considered God's commands to be a burden. On the contrary, he delighted in them (v. 35). Jesus and His Word are so connected that we can't love one and disregard the other. If we love Jesus, we will obey His Word.

> *Close your time asking God to give you a heart that loves Him above all things. Ask Him to increase your desire for Him and to give you a delight for the Scriptures.*

Personal Study 2
COUNTERFEIT OR AUTHENTIC?

As seen in the previous personal study, there is a kind of belief that Jesus doesn't recognize as saving faith. When we love and trust Jesus, we obey Him (John 14:15). Today, we'll look at additional passages that reveal what saving faith looks like. In Matthew's Gospel, Jesus differentiated between counterfeit and authentic faith.

> *Beware of false prophets, who come to you in sheep's clothing but inwardly are ravenous wolves. You will recognize them by their fruits. Are grapes gathered from thornbushes, or figs from thistles? So, every healthy tree bears good fruit, but the diseased tree bears bad fruit. A healthy tree cannot bear bad fruit, nor can a diseased tree bear good fruit.*
> MATTHEW 7:15-18

In your own words, what is a wolf in sheep's clothing?

How would you describe the difference between good fruit and bad fruit?

How do these metaphors help us identify the motives of people?

Jesus taught that God's people will be confronted with people who present themselves to be godly, but in reality, they are dangerous predators intent to do harm. Jesus said we could tell if they are genuine or not by how they behave. Certainly, it's wise to listen to what people have to say. But if what someone says isn't backed up by the way they live, something is wrong. Authentic faith is represented by consistency between words and actions.

How can you tell the difference between someone who makes a mistake and someone who consistently bears bad fruit?

Why is it sometimes difficult to admit someone is not who you thought them to be?

Loving God Means Loving People

Saving faith in Jesus Christ influences how we live. If someone claims to be a Christian yet no evidence of that manifests itself in their character over a long period of time, there is reason for concern. We need to keep in mind that people don't start in the same place and therefore we can't expect people to reach spiritual maturity at the same rate. However, we can expect there to be signs of change. Jesus taught there are specific indicators that accompany genuine faith. Just before going to the cross, Jesus told His disciples how the world would know we belong to Him:

A new commandment I give to you, that you love one another: just as I have loved you, you also are to love one another. By this all people will know that you are my disciples, if you have love for one another.
JOHN 13:34-35

What does it mean to love others the way Jesus has loved us?

Do you think most Christians are known for their love for each other? Why or why not?

Who in your friend group or student ministry can you demonstrate the love of Christ to this week?

Jesus didn't say the world would recognize a Christ-follower by his or her GPA, neighborhood, material possessions, number of followers, or social status. He said the world would recognize we belonged to Him if we loved each other in the same way He has loved us. Evidence of saving faith reveals itself in love for God, obedience to His Word, and love for one another (John 13:34-35; 14:15). If you want to know if someone truly loves Jesus, take a look at their life and their love.

> *Close your time in prayer by asking God to deepen your love for Him and for other people. Give thanks for the gift of saving faith.*

Born of the Spirit

GROUP STUDY

Start
Welcome everyone to session 10.

All of us fill roles in other people's lives. We are sons and daughters, brothers and sisters, friends and neighbors. Our relationships contain similarities, but they also have differences depending on the context. In this session, we'll be introduced to a man named Nicodemus. Nicodemus approached Jesus as a rabbi and great teacher, and Jesus was a rabbi and a great teacher. However, we'll see why Jesus fills a far more significant role than those titles.

What are some of the ways you have approached Jesus?

To prepare for video session 10, pray that God will help each person understand and apply this truth:

Those who are born of the Spirit practice repentance by turning away from sin and turning toward Christ.

Watch

Use the space below to take notes
while you watch video session 10.

Discuss

*Use the following questions to guide
your discussion of the video.*

1. Nicodemus approached Jesus as a rabbi and teacher. Even though this was true, what was Nicodemus missing about Jesus?

2. John 3:1-8 teaches that we must be "born again" and relate to Him in the Spirit. Why is the concept of being "born again" difficult for some people to accept?

3. To be born again we must repent. Pastor Matt defined repentance as "turning from sin to know, love, trust, and obey Jesus." Why does repentance have to be a lifestyle rather than a one-time event?

4. Why is belief and faith, like repentance, a continuous act that must be chosen over and over? What does this look like in your daily life?

A MAN NAMED NICODEMUS

Read John 3:1-8.

What was Nicodemus' standing among the Jews? Why does this matter?

What seems to have led Nicodemus to visit Jesus? Why did he come at night?

Nicodemus was a man in high-standing among the leaders of Israel and would have been considered a member of the religious elite. He was also a theologian and a "teacher of Israel" (v. 10). Nicodemus was a man who had likely spent a lot of time studying the Old Testament Scriptures, and yet he didn't understand what Jesus was teaching him, and he didn't recognize Jesus as the Messiah. Jesus was causing a lot of talk among the Pharisees, so it's not surprising Nicodemus chose to visit Jesus. Because Nicodemus visited Jesus at night, it's possible he didn't want people to know, or perhaps he wanted to question Jesus privately.

Nicodemus said "Rabbi, we know that you are a teacher come from God..." (v. 2). Do you think that Nicodemus was speaking for himself or the religious group he represented?

What other elements of Jesus' identity was Nicodemus missing?

How do our own assumptions and understanding about Jesus impact the way we relate to Him?

You Must Be Born Again

The religious rulers of the Jews had concerns about Jesus. He had been the topic of much discussion, but Nicodemus' words were diplomatic. He even went as far as to acknowledge that Jesus was a gifted teacher of God (v. 2). But Jesus didn't even acknowledge Nicodemus' statement. Instead, Jesus got straight to the point. Jesus answered him, "Truly, truly, I say to you, unless one is born again he cannot see the kingdom of God" (John 3:3).

What comes to mind when you hear the term "born again"?

Nicodemus couldn't get past the literal idea of being born again. Jesus was talking about spiritual things. How would you describe what it means to spiritually be born again to a non-believer?

Why do you think Jesus redirected Nicodemus so quickly?

Water and Spirit

Jesus wasn't interested in Nicodemus' flattering statement. Remember, Jesus knows what's in the heart of all people (John 2:25). Jesus knew Nicodemus lacked saving faith, and so Jesus explained that in addition to our natural birth, people must experience a spiritual rebirth to become children of God and members of His kingdom. Nicodemus didn't understand what Jesus was saying and told Him as much (v. 4). But Jesus didn't simplify it or back down. To be born of water and the Spirit means we have been spiritually transformed and given inward renewal that can only come from God's transforming work in our lives.

In verse 8, Jesus compared the Holy Spirit to the "wind." Why is this a fitting analogy?

What role does the Holy Spirit play in being born again?

To be a Christian, Jesus said we must be born again through the Holy Spirit. Jesus compared the Spirit to wind. The wind is invisible, but you can see the effects of it. In the same way, the Spirit is invisible but the effects are obvious. All believers have the Holy Spirit (Gal. 4:6). He is the agent that brings transformation and renewal to our lives.

Close your time in prayer by giving thanks to God for the gift of spiritual rebirth and the forgiveness of sins.

Personal Study 2
LIFE IN THE SPIRIT

For all who are led by the Spirit of God are sons of God.
ROMANS 8:14

In the previous personal study, we mentioned that the Holy Spirit is like a blowing wind. We are meant to be encouraged by watching the wind of the Spirit move in the lives of God's people. What does that look like? When you open up the Bible and read it, when you gather with others in the name of Jesus, when you choose right over wrong because you love Jesus, these are all examples—and so much more—of what it looks like for the wind of the Spirit to blow in your life.

When are you most mindful of the Spirit's work in your life?

List some of the specific ways you've seen "the wind blowing" in other people's lives.

How have you seen the Spirit work in your life recently?

The Role of the Holy Spirit

Look up the following passages and write down what these Scriptures reveal about the Holy Spirit.

John 16:8-11

Romans 8:14

Romans 8:26

Acts 20:22-23

What new insights did you learn from these passages?

The Holy Spirit remains a mystery to many believers, and because we are so unfamiliar with His roles, we miss Him and fail to see evidence of His work in our lives. But when we are born again and become children of God, the Holy Spirit becomes an integral part of our lives. The Holy Spirit has been given to us to help us in the practical matters of day-to-day living. Jesus knew we would need a Helper, and He gave us one (John 14:26).

In what ways have you been guilty of ignoring the Holy Spirit's presence in your life?

After reading the Scripture passages, can you identify things the Holy Spirit has done in your life where you haven't given Him adequate credit?

A Helper

Jesus offered a simple description of the Holy Spirit—a Helper:

> *Nevertheless, I tell you the truth: it is to your advantage*
> *that I go away, for if I do not go away, the Helper will*
> *not come to you. But if I go, I will send him to you.*
> **JOHN 16:7**

Why would Jesus leaving be to the disciples' advantage?

How is the Holy Spirit a Helper?

What outcome or situations can you attribute to the power of the Holy Spirit in your life today?

Just before going to the cross, Jesus gathered His disciples, and one of the things He told them to anticipate was the Holy Spirit. Jesus understands that we need the power of God to live the Christian life because we can't do it on our own. If we didn't need help, there would've been no need to send a Helper—but He did. The Christian life is not simply difficult—it is impossible apart from the Holy Spirit. And God doesn't expect us to attempt it apart from the power of the Spirit.

> *Close your time in prayer giving thanks to God*
> *for giving the gift of the Holy Spirit.*

A Love That Gives and Sends

GROUP STUDY

Start
Welcome everyone to session 11.

People are enthralled with the concept of love. In every generation, love has been the topic of countless books, songs, sappy social media posts, and movies. People can't get enough of it. Interestingly, the concept of love is the focus of the most well-known passage in the New Testament: "For God so loved the world, that he gave his only Son, that whoever believes in him should not perish but have eternal life (John 3:16).

How does our world depict love?

Do you think it's an accurate picture? Why or why not?

To prepare for video session 11, pray that God will help each person understand and apply this truth:

Jesus' mission to seek and save sinners reveals the love of God that gives and sends freely and fully.

Watch

Use the space below to take notes
while you watch video session 11.

Discuss
*Use the following questions to guide
your discussion of the video.*

1. What are some ways we mistakenly believe our religious behavior is enough to get us into heaven? Why is this not true?

2. Why is it impossible for us to see our need for redemption if we don't understand the magnitude of our sin problem?

3. The words "trust and believe" are used 241 times throughout the New Testament, 98 times just within the Gospel of John. Why do you think it is a theme we see over and over?

4. If you are a believer, what might it look like for you to "be sent" to share the gospel with other people?

5. Who were the people who were instrumental in telling you about Jesus and teaching you what it means to be a Christian? How could you model that same service to other people?

HOW CAN THESE THINGS BE?

In the last session, we spent time exploring a conversation between Jesus and Nicodemus. Nicodemus was a religious man—a Pharisee, and member of the Sanhedrin. By that day's standards, Nicodemus was considered a member of the religious elite. But Jesus told Nicodemus that religious standing isn't enough to get anyone into the kingdom of God—we must be born again (John 3:3). Today, we'll pick up midway through the conversation.

Read John 3:9-15.

Nicodemus lacked understanding and asked, "How can these things be?" Jesus rebuked him but also had compassion and took time to explain things. What does this reveal to us about the heart of Christ?

When have you experienced God's compassion in your life?

Merciful Judgment

Nicodemus didn't understand what Jesus was saying so Jesus directed their conversation to a story about the Israelites found in the Book of Numbers. God had delivered the people from slavery in Egypt, and provided for their needs, but as they traveled back to Canaan, the people complained and were impatient with God and Moses. Their attitude and behavior demonstrated rebellion and God responded in judgment by sending a plague of poisonous snakes (Num. 21:4-6). God's judgment had it's intended effect and the people repented of their wicked behavior. When God saw that the people had repented, He responded in mercy.

"And the Lord said to Moses, 'Make a fiery serpent and set it on a pole, and everyone who is bitten, when he sees it, shall live.'" (Num. 21:8).

How was God's act of judgment ultimately an act of mercy?

Why does it sometimes take difficult circumstances to motivate us to repent?

What was Jesus' ultimate point in telling this story about the bronze serpent to Nicodemus?

The Son of Man Must Be Lifted Up

Jesus told this story to Nicodemus to make a comparison. When Jesus used the phrase, "lifted up" He was speaking to the fact that He would be lifted up on a cross. For people to become children of God, and to enter His kingdom, He would have to take on the sting of death and suffer the pain of the cross.

Glance back to John 3:15. What is the outcome for those who believe in the Son of Man?

What is the outcome for those who fail to believe?

Why is it so easy for us, like Nicodemus, to confuse religious behavior and biblical knowledge for saving faith?

John also wrote in 1 John 5:12, "Whoever has the Son has life; whoever does not have the Son of God does not have life." How does this verse prove that there are not multiple paths to God?

Jesus explained that He would be "lifted up" on a cross so that "whoever believes in him may have eternal life" (3:15). Jesus' point parallels the Israelites in the wilderness. Those who had suffered from snakebites were going to die, but God gave them a remedy to prevent their destruction (21:8). In Jesus' teaching to Nicodemus, He revealed that because of sin, all of humanity is in a deadly spiritual state. Our only cure for sin is to look to Jesus and His work on the cross. Only in looking to Jesus can we be saved from our sin.

> *Close your time in prayer, giving thanks to God for providing*
> *a remedy in Jesus Christ for our fatal spiritual condition.*

Personal Study 2

FOR GOD SO LOVED THE WORLD

Read John 3:16-21.

Without a doubt, John 3:16 is the most well-known passages in the New Testament. It's seen on T-shirts, bumper stickers, and written on signs in the stands at professional sporting events. Sadly, it's also a passage that is frequently taken out of context.

> *For God so loved the world, that he gave his only Son, that whoever believes in him should not perish but have eternal life.*
> **JOHN 3:16**

Restate John 3:16 in the simplest form:

Some people read John 3:16 and come to the false conclusion that God offers salvation to everyone regardless of what they believe or who they worship. They believe all paths lead to God. In our world, some would assert that if God really were loving He would have provided a variety of options. But God didn't provide a variety of options—He provided One. The text says that God's love is so deep that He sent His only Son. True belief is conditioned upon belief in the Son.

Why do you think people get angry when they hear there is only one way to God?

How does the sense of injustice some feel when they learn Jesus is the only way reveal a lack of understanding about our sin nature?

For God did not send his Son into the world to condemn the world, but in order that the world might be saved through him. Whoever believes in him is not condemned, but whoever does not believe is condemned already, because he has not believed in the name of the only Son of God.
JOHN 3:17-18

What was God's reason for sending His Son?

Those who believe in Jesus aren't condemned. What is the alternative for those who don't believe? Why should this lead us to tell others about Jesus with urgency?

Jesus' mission in coming to this world was to save people. Those who believe in Jesus and trust His work on the cross for their salvation will not be condemned. But those who refuse Christ are condemned because there is no other option for being reconciled to God. Apart from Jesus, we live in darkness. John wrote, "And this is the judgment: the light has come into the world, and people loved the darkness rather than the light because their works were evil" (John 3:19).

No Other Name

*And there is salvation in no one else, for there is no other name
under heaven given among men by which we must be saved.*
ACTS 4:12

Why is the lie of "there are many ways to heaven" so prevalent?

**In John 14:6 Jesus said, "I am the way, and the truth, and the life.
No one comes to the Father except through me." What is your response
to the reality that there is only one way?**

Who do you need to share the saving plan of God with this week?

God didn't send His sinless Son to die on a cross so He could be one among
many paths to salvation. Jesus is the only path. God's motivation was love: it's
a love given to us that sends us into the world to tell our friends and neighbors
about the only love that saves. When we freely receive the gift of salvation, it is
our joy to share it with others.

> *Close your time in prayer giving thanks to God that there is no
> condemnation for those who believe in Jesus. Ask Him to lead
> you to people who need to hear the good news of the gospel.*

SESSION 12

Our Place and Message

GROUP STUDY

Start
Welcome everyone to session 12.

We live in a consumer-driven culture where customer satisfaction is most important. If a company doesn't meet our needs, we take our business elsewhere. In a consumer-driven society, it's natural and even appropriate for business owners to compete. But a competitor's mindset has no place in the church. If we belong to Jesus, it's our calling to work together for the kingdom of God with other believers. Our job is to collectively point as many people to Jesus as possible.

What would it look like for churches to work together to serve the kingdom of God?

To prepare for video session 12, pray that God will help each person understand and apply this truth:

We pursue gospel-centered multiplication to point as many people as possible to Jesus.

Watch

*Use the space below to take notes
while you watch video session 12.*

     Video sessions available at lifeway.com/johnbiblestudy

Discuss

*Use the following questions to guide
your discussion of the video.*

1. In the video teaching, Pastor Matt's two points were that "we need to know our place and our message." How would you describe your place and the message you've been given?

2. How would you describe the difference between an allegiance to Jesus versus an allegiance to your own desires? How can your desires merge with your allegiance to Jesus?

3. Pastor Matt said "Our place is to be happy under the sovereign reign of God." How does being happy serving God reduce our desire for infighting and competition with other believers?

4. Why is it wrong for churches to compete with each other? What is the godly response when we see another church or ministry succeed?

5. If we truly believe Jesus is above all and over all, how will it be obvious in the ways we relate to other people?

Personal Study 1

JESUS ABOVE ALL

In this final session, we'll look at a conversation between John the Baptist and his disciples. We'll see that when we know our place and message we experience great joy when the kingdom of God advances.

Read John 3:22-36.

Why were John the Baptist's disciples concerned about Jesus' ministry (v. 26)?

In what areas are you prone to envy? How do you act when you feel envious?

Were the concerns of John's disciples natural or selfish? Explain why you feel the way you do.

I Am Not the Christ

John the Baptist and his disciples were baptizing people in the Judean countryside when John's disciples noticed that more and more people were going to Jesus to be baptized rather than John (v. 26). Andrew, Peter's brother, had already left John to follow Jesus (1:35-41), but John still had a group of disciples who continued to travel with him. These men were loyal to John and felt threatened when they realized their ministry was losing momentum. The situation bothered them so much they brought it to John's attention. John responded in a noteworthy manner:

You yourselves bear me witness, that I said, 'I am not the Christ, but I have been sent before him.' The one who has the bride is the bridegroom. The friend of the bridegroom, who stands and hears him, rejoices greatly at the bridegroom's voice. Therefore this joy of mine is now complete. He must increase, but I must decrease.
JOHN 3:28-30

Why did John welcome the success of Jesus' ministry?

John said, "He must increase, but I must decrease." Why is this statement true for everyone who follows Jesus?

Joy That Is Complete

From the beginning, John the Baptist had identified himself as "the voice of one crying in the wilderness" (Matt. 3:3) who would prepare people for the coming of the Lord. John was sent as the forerunner to Jesus so he gladly embraced Christ's arrival. John had been pointing people to Jesus and his ministry was bearing fruit. To explain, John used the analogy of the groom and the best man (3:29). John pointed out that the bride (the church) didn't belong to him—it belonged to Jesus. But John felt great joy in seeing things unfold and said, "Therefore this joy of mine is now complete" (3:29b).

Why could John experience joy even as his ministry was winding down?

How does this passage reveal that John the Baptist understood his place in the kingdom?

Even as John's ministry began to wind down, do you think he had been faithful to his calling? Why or why not?

When we live with the mindset that "Jesus is above all," how can we be content and even happy when another person, church, or ministry experiences a win for the kingdom of God?

The best antidote for spiritual envy is to trust in the sovereignty of God. Trust Him in seasons of success and failure. Trust that He knows the proper times and places for everything. Just be faithful to follow His lead and give Him the glory. John the Baptist understood his role as a forerunner who would prepare people for Jesus' coming. Knowing his place freed John to rejoice in the Father's sovereign plan. When we acknowledge Jesus above all, we will have complete joy when we see His kingdom advancing.

> *Close your time in prayer by asking God to show you your place in ministry. Give thanks that in His sovereign plan He asks His people to build His kingdom.*

Personal Study 2
HE MUST INCREASE

He must increase, but I must decrease.
JOHN 3:30

In the previous day, we discussed a conversation between John and his disciples who were concerned that Jesus' ministry was surpassing John's. In this conversation, John spoke the most well-known words to ever be uttered from his mouth: "He must increase, but I must decrease" (3:30). John's calling was to go before Jesus and announce His coming, and then fade into the background as Jesus emerged as the Son of God and long-awaited Messiah.

Read John 3:31-36.

According to John, what was Jesus' status (v. 31)?

How did John's view of Jesus "above all" inform his life and ministry?

John made a series of statements about Jesus. In your own words, how would you summarize what he said?

His Place and His Message

John the Baptist understood his place and his message because he had come to terms with Jesus' place and message. He said, "He who comes from above is above all" (John 3:31a). Only when we get that right can everything else fall in correct order. John knew Jesus had come from the Father and had come to Earth with a message and was declaring the very words of God.

Think about your own life for a moment. Do you live with an awareness that Jesus is above all? Why or why not?

What would have to change for your life to demonstrate that Jesus is above all?

The Spirit Without Measure

For he whom God has sent utters the words of God, for he gives the Spirit without measure.
JOHN 3:34

In our quest to live lives that exalt Jesus above all, these words should encourage us. God doesn't give the Spirit in partial measure but immeasurably. This is beautiful news for those of us who feel stagnant, confused, trapped in cycles of addiction, or in broken ways of thinking. We don't have to be stuck within the boundaries of our broken limitations—we get the Spirit without measure. The Spirit empowers us to live spiritually vibrant lives that bring glory to God and do things we could never accomplish in our own strength. When we rely on the Holy

Spirit to strengthen and empower us we have the ability to obey God, fulfill our callings, and live a life we could never bring to pass in our own effort.

What is something you need the Holy Spirit's help with to enable you to do what you can't do in your own strength?

On a scale of 1 to 10 (10 being the most mindful; 1 being the least), how mindful are you that the Holy Spirit is an ever-present help and that God gives the Spirit without measure?

Think for a moment about the new things you've learned during the last 12 sessions. What stands out to you?

As our time in John 1-3 comes to a close, let's remind ourselves of John's reason for writing— "Now Jesus did many other signs in the presence of the disciples, which are not written in this book; but these are written so that you may believe that Jesus is the Christ, the Son of God, and that by believing you may have life in his name" (John 20:30-31). As we conclude, let's remain mindful that the starting point in the Christian life is believing that Jesus is the Son of God—but it doesn't stop there. The Christian life is a life of believing—and having life in His name.

> *Give thanks to God for the new insights you've learned from John's Gospel. Ask Him to give you the Spirit without measure. Pray He will equip you to live with the mindset that Jesus is above all.*

John 1-3
LEADER GUIDE

1. PRAYERFULLY PREPARE

Prepare for each group session with prayer. Ask the Holy Spirit to work through you and the group discussion as you point to Jesus each week through God's Word.

2. ENCOURAGE DISCUSSION

A good small-group experience has the following characteristics.

EVERYONE PARTICIPATES. Encourage everyone to ask questions, share responses, or read aloud.

NO ONE DOMINATES—NOT EVEN THE LEADER. Be sure your time speaking as a leader takes up less than half your time together as a group. Politely guide discussion if anyone dominates.

DON'T RUSH THROUGH QUESTIONS. Don't feel that a moment of silence is a bad thing. Students often need time to think about their responses to questions they've just heard or to gain courage to share what God is stirring in their hearts.

AFFIRM AND FOLLOW UP ON INPUT. Make sure you point out something true or helpful in a response. Don't just move on. Build community with follow-up questions, asking how other students have experienced similar things or how a truth has shaped their understanding of God and the Scripture you're studying.

KEEP GOD AND HIS WORD CENTRAL. Opinions and experiences can be helpful, but God has given us the truth. Trust Scripture to be the authority and God's Spirit to work in student's lives. You can't change anyone, but God can. Continually point people to the Word and to active steps of faith.

3. KEEP CONNECTING

Think of ways to connect with students during the week. Participation during the group session always improves when members spend time connecting with one another outside the group sessions. The more people are comfortable with one another the more they'll look forward to being together.

Encourage students with thoughts, commitments, or questions from the session by connecting through texts and/or social media. Build deeper connection by planning or spontaneously inviting students to get together outside your regularly scheduled group time for a meal, fun activities, fellowships, and/or projects around your church or community.

4. LEAD GROUP SESSIONS

Thank you for being willing to lead a group of students through an in-depth study of *John 1-3*. If this is your first time leading a group, don't overthink it. Prepare to lead by viewing the video session, reading the suggestions for the group session, and completing the personal study each week. Be prepared to distribute Bible-study books and to show each video session. For session 1 you'll want to familiarize students with the format of the study, including the way the group session will be structured ("Start," "Watch," "Discuss") and the features of the Bible-study book (two personal studies each week). In addition, use the following guides to help you prepare for the group sessions.

Group Session 1

START

The following is an optional ice-breaker question/activity. Feel free to use or adapt in a way that works well for your students.

Ask participants to introduce themselves with quick answers to the following question: What's one phrase, nickname, or fact that summarizes who you are?

WATCH

As a group, watch the Session 1 video and encourage students to take notes as they watch.

DISCUSS

Session 1 introduces the study of John's Gospel. John wrote His Gospel so people would believe that Jesus is the Son of God and by believing they would find life in His name (John 20:31). John opened his prologue by immediately revealing Jesus' identity. Spend time discussing why knowing what you believe about Jesus' identity is foundational to the Christian faith.

Explain that each time the group meets, you'll start the session by reviewing the previous week's topic. Your review will follow the outline of the video session and personal study. Emphasize the importance of engaging with the Scriptures throughout the week.

Group Session 2

REVIEW

Beginning this week, you'll start each group session by reviewing the previous week's study. Make sure to manage the time well, allowing time to discuss the teaching after the video.

START

The following is an optional ice-breaker question/activity. Feel free to use or adapt in a way that works well for your students.

Give every student a strip of paper. Then direct them to write something they believe on the strip of paper, like "Cats are a better pet than dogs" or "Iron Man is cooler than Captain America." Allow each student to read their strip of paper and give each one 30 seconds to defend their belief. After they finish their defense ask, "How did you come to believe this?"

Was anyone's mind changed by these defenses? What prompted your change of thinking?

WATCH

As a group, watch the Session 2 video and encourage students to take notes as they watch.

DISCUSS

This session focuses on the topic of God-given belief. The primary goal of this lesson should be to discuss how God initiates and sustains our faith.

Group Session 3

REVIEW

Review the previous week's study. Make sure to manage the time well, allowing time to discuss the teaching after the video.

START

The following is an optional ice-breaker question/activity. Feel free to use or adapt in a way that works well for your students.

Play a game a musical chairs. Arrange chairs in a circle, with one less than the number of people playing. Then direct students to sit down in a chair when the music stops. Whoever is left without a chair is eliminated from the game. Play until there is only one person remaining.

How did you feel as you were walking around the circle of chairs listening for the music to stop? Explain.

WATCH

As a group, watch the Session 3 video and encourage students to take notes as they watch.

DISCUSS

This week focuses on God's grace. God gives us the faith to believe and that is the starting point of the Christian life. Encourage group members to identify specific ways God has given them grace and encourage them to talk about ways they are relying on God's grace in the future.

Group Session 4

REVIEW

Review the previous week's study. Make sure to manage the time well, allowing time to discuss the teaching after the video.

START

The following is an optional ice-breaker question/activity. Feel free to use or adapt in a way that works well for your students.

Play a round of "2 Truths and 1 Lie" with your group. Allow each student to present their two truths and one lie and see if the rest of the group can pick out which one is the lie.

Why did you pick these two truths? Why did you pick the one as a lie? What do these things say about you?

WATCH

As a group, watch the Session 4 video and encourage students to take notes as they watch.

DISCUSS

Spend time discussing how we can only know who we are by understanding our identity in Jesus. Emphasize the reality that due to our continued struggle with our sin nature, grasping the truth of our identity in Christ is a lifelong process.

Group Session 5

REVIEW

Review the previous week's study. Make sure to manage the time well, allowing time to discuss the teaching after the video.

START

The following is an optional ice-breaker question/activity. Feel free to use or adapt in a way that works well for your students.

> **Play a game of "Six Degrees of Separation." List two actors who have not been in a movie or TV show together, and without the aid of smart phones or the Internet, see if you can connect them to each other within six moves. For example, connect Chris Pratt to Tom Hanks. Pratt was in *Jurassic World* with Bryce Dallas Howard, whose father is Ron Howard, who directed Tom Hanks in *Splash*.**

WATCH

As a group, watch the Session 5 video and encourage students to take notes as they watch.

DISCUSS

Spend time discussing what it means to abide in Jesus. Encourage students to identify ways they can prioritize abiding in Jesus above everything else.

Group Session 6

REVIEW

Review the previous week's study. Make sure to manage the time well, allowing time to discuss the teaching after the video.

START

The following is an optional ice-breaker question/activity. Feel free to use or adapt in a way that works well for your students.

Invite the first student who can produce a form of identification to play a game. Make three envelopes with small prizes in them like a one dollar bill, a gift card with only change left on it, a coupon for 20% off at Bed, Bath & Beyond, and so on. Invite the student to choose an envelope, then give them the option to keep their envelope or trade it for a wrapped box with a similar type of prize inside. Repeat this cycle until the student chooses a prize, then invite them to open it.

How did you decide which gift to accept that you were invited to receive?

WATCH

As a group, watch the Session 6 video and encourage students to take notes as they watch.

DISCUSS

Discuss the difference between merely believing God's exists and following Him as Lord. Encourage students to think about whether or not they are willing to follow Jesus on His terms rather than their own. Share that the better we know Jesus the more we trust Him. Discuss why following Jesus is worth the cost.

Group Session 7

REVIEW

Review the previous week's study. Make sure to manage the time well, allowing time to discuss the teaching after the video.

START

The following is an optional ice-breaker question/activity. Feel free to use or adapt in a way that works well for your students.

Many adults are baffled by how students learn to do math today. Write a basic math problem on a whiteboard or tear sheet and ask students to show the different ways they've learned to solve the problem.

What are the challenges that come with a new way of doing things?

WATCH

As a group, watch the Session 7 video and encourage students to take notes as they watch.

DISCUSS

Discuss that Jesus' first miracle represents the reality that the old way had passed and a new way had come. Encourage group members to identify ways their relationships with others are impacted because of their relationship with Jesus.

Group Session 8

REVIEW

Review the previous week's study. Make sure to manage the time well, allowing time to discuss the teaching after the video.

START

The following is an optional ice-breaker question/activity. Feel free to use or adapt in a way that works well for your students.

Take a moment and go around the group and ask students what job they desire in their future. Ask: "Why do you want to do that job when you're older?"

What types of things do you need to know about someone to feel confident that you know them well?

WATCH

As a group, watch the Session 8 video and encourage students to take notes as they watch.

DISCUSS

What John was trying to do in this gospel account was not just reveal what Jesus does; but who He is. 1) Jesus is a prophet who challenges the spiritual consumer. 2) He is a priest who cleanses us from sin. 3) He is a king who builds a temple for God's presence. Spend time discussing who Jesus is with students.

Group Session 9

REVIEW

Review the previous week's study. Make sure to manage the time well, allowing time to discuss the teaching after the video.

START

The following is an optional ice-breaker question/activity. Feel free to use or adapt in a way that works well for your students.

Ask for a volunteer who would be willing to do an impersonation of a famous person or singer. See if the rest of the group can figure out whose famous voice they are trying to impersonate.

Who is your favorite actor, singer, or athlete? What do you like about them?

WATCH

As a group, watch the Session 9 video and encourage students to take notes as they watch.

DISCUSS

Today's verses state there are men and women who believed in Jesus, but Jesus, did not entrust Himself to them. The kind of belief that is not saving belief is when we believe that we can make God our errand boy to get us what we really want rather than to be our Lord and Savior. Ask group members to assess the nature of their belief.

Group Session 10

REVIEW

Review the previous week's study. Make sure to manage the time well, allowing time to discuss the teaching after the video.

START

The following is an optional ice-breaker question/activity. Feel free to use or adapt in a way that works well for your students.

Play a version of "The Newlywed Game." Students will need further explanation since this is a very old game show. Guide students who are friends to pair up, then ask them the same three questions, such as "What is your friend's favorite color?" or "What is your friend's birthday?" Instruct students to record their answers on paper, then ask them to reveal their answers to see if they match.

How do your relationships differ depending on the context? For example, how might your relationship with your parents be different than with your friends?

WATCH

As a group, watch the Session 10 video and encourage students to take notes as they watch.

DISCUSS

Discuss with students how 1) Jesus is more than a teacher; He's our Savior. 2) We must be born again of water and Spirit, not just flesh. 3) We must believe.

Group Session 11

REVIEW

Review the previous week's study. Make sure to manage the time well, allowing time to discuss the teaching after the video.

START

The following is an optional ice-breaker question/activity. Feel free to use or adapt in a way that works well for your students.

> **Compile a list of 5-10 ideas students will have strong reactions to, such as "pineapple on pizza is delicious," "Nintendo Switch is more fun than Xbox," and "Disney World is overrated." Direct students to stand if they love the statement and remain sitting if they do not.**

> **When you love someone or something, how do you show it?**

WATCH

As a group, watch the Session 11 video and encourage students to take notes as they watch.

DISCUSS

This session's focal point: One can only enter the kingdom through belief in the saving work the Son came to do. His mission that was a consequence of the love of the Father—a love that gives and sends, fully and freely, to save and redeem.

Group Session 12

REVIEW

Review the previous week's study. Since this is the final week of the study, ask students what they will carry with them from these past 12 weeks.

START

The following is an optional ice-breaker question/activity. Feel free to use or adapt in a way that works well for your students.

> Write out a list of six local restaurants, like Chick-Fil-A®, Wendy's®, McDonald's®, and so on. Ask each student to rank them from 6 (worst) to 1 (best). Then give a few students the chance to explain why they chose them in the order they did.

> What are specific ways these restaurants compete with one another?

WATCH

As a group, watch the Session 12 video and encourage students to take notes as they watch.

DISCUSS

Our final session can be summarized in two points: 1) When we say, "We know our place," what we're saying is God is up to something, and our job is to happily join Him in what He's doing. 2) Simply put, our message is Jesus is above all.

NOTES